PEANUTS®

SNOOPY,
First Beagle on the Moon!

by Charles M. Schulz
adapted by Ximena Hastings
illustrated by Robert Pope

Ready-to-Read

Simon Spotlight
New York   London   Toronto   Sydney   New Delhi

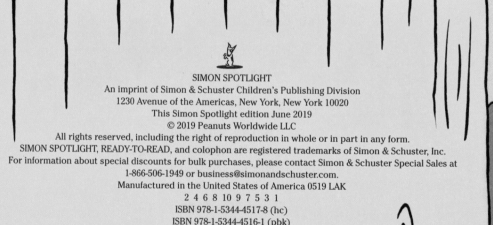

SIMON SPOTLIGHT
An imprint of Simon & Schuster Children's Publishing Division
1230 Avenue of the Americas, New York, New York 10020
This Simon Spotlight edition June 2019
© 2019 Peanuts Worldwide LLC
SIMON SPOTLIGHT, READY-TO-READ, and colophon are registered trademarks of Simon & Schuster, Inc.
For information about special discounts for bulk purchases, please contact Simon & Schuster Special Sales at
1-866-506-1949 or business@simonandschuster.com.
Manufactured in the United States of America 0519 LAK
2 4 6 8 10 9 7 5 3 1
ISBN 978-1-5344-4517-8 (hc)
ISBN 978-1-5344-4516-1 (pbk)
ISBN 978-1-5344-4518-5 (eBook)

Snoopy, the world-famous astronaut,
has a mission.
He is going to travel into space
and find water on the moon!

First, Snoopy must prepare
for his trip.
"I need to wear a space helmet,"
Snoopy tells Woodstock.

Woodstock hands him a baseball cap.
"Well, yes . . . sort of like that,"
Snoopy says.

Snoopy finds a real space helmet
and a space suit.
He also packs some snacks.

Next, Snoopy does a safety check
on his doghouse.
Safety is always the most important
part of a mission!

Finally, Snoopy sits on his doghouse
and prepares for launch.
"All systems are go!" he says.

Woodstock chirps at Snoopy.
Snoopy understands him perfectly.
"Okay!" Snoopy says. "I will bring back
a present from the moon for you!"

Woodstock chirps the countdown.
Three!
Two!
One!

We have liftoff!

Snoopy launches higher and higher
into the sky.
The view is beautiful!

After a while, Snoopy lands safely
on the moon.

"I did it!
I'm the first beagle on the moon!"
Snoopy says.
"I beat everybody. I even beat
that cat who lives next door!"

Then Snoopy sees someone
walking toward him.
Who is it?
Could it be . . . an alien?

It is not an alien.
It is his brother Spike!

The brothers are thrilled
to see each other.

"Are we on the moon?" Snoopy asks.
"I thought you lived in Needles."
Spike does not know.
But he does know that
his shop sells a snow globe
with a moon inside!

Snoopy buys the snow globe.
It will make a nice gift
for Woodstock.

Spike joins Snoopy
on his mission.

Spike finds a strange rock.

Snoopy collects dust.

They cannot find any water, though.

After a while,
Snoopy and Spike are tired.
They decide to take a break
and eat some dog treats.

Snoopy wants to picnic
inside a shiny crater.
Then he looks more closely.
The crater is covered in ice.

"Ice is frozen water,"
says Snoopy. "I did it!
I found water on the moon!"

"My shop sells water bottles,
you know," Spike says,
but Snoopy tells him water bottles
and ice are not the same thing.

Snoopy collects some ice samples.
Now his mission is complete.
He says goodbye to Spike
and begins his return to Earth.

*Here is the world-famous astronaut
returning from the moon,
239 thousand miles through space!*
Snoopy thinks.

Then Snoopy's stomach grumbles.
He realizes that Earth is still
very far away.
What if he misses dinner?

After a while, Snoopy lands safely
in Charlie Brown's backyard.
Woodstock loves the snow globe!

Snoopy's stomach grumbles again.
Then Charlie Brown opens the door.
"Snoopy, it's dinnertime!"
he calls.

"I gave you a little extra food,"
Charlie Brown says.
"I thought you might be hungry
after exploring the moon."

It's good to be back home,
Snoopy thinks.
Just in time for dinner!

Turn the page to learn more about the moon, Snoopy's space gear, and the long relationship between Peanuts and NASA!

THE MOON

The Earth's moon is the biggest and brightest object in the night sky. The moon orbits, or circles around, the Earth about every twenty-eight days.

Fun Moon Facts

- The moon is about 239,000 miles away from the Earth, but the actual distance is always changing. That's a long way!
- The moon's surface has many craters, which are large round dents made from other objects having crashed into it.
- Moonlight is actually just sunlight being reflected off the moon's surface.
- You can often see the moon in the sky during daytime, too.
- The temperature on the moon can get hotter than 250 degrees Fahrenheit and as cold as negative 400 degrees Fahrenheit.

Humans on the Moon!

In July 1969, NASA's *Apollo 11* spacecraft landed on the moon's surface. People all around the world watched as astronauts Neil Armstrong and Buzz Aldrin became the first humans to walk on the moon. Since then ten more people have walked on the moon so far.

Is There Water on the Moon?

NASA has confirmed there is water ice on the moon's surface. In 2018, a team of scientists found evidence at the moon's poles. This discovery might help astronauts live on the moon one day.

SNOOPY'S SPACE SUIT

Space is full of wonders and mysteries. Snoopy's space suit and helmet keep him safe on any adventure that comes his way!

The space suit is made up of many layers, each with their own purpose. A space suit arm has fourteen layers!

The suit gloves include little heaters so Snoopy's paws do not get cold.

The suit comes with a drink bag and a "straw" so Snoopy can drink water without taking off his suit.

The Primary Life Support System (PLSS) looks like a backpack. It carries a battery and a fan that helps supply oxygen to Snoopy. It also has a radio.

The space helmet provides oxygen to breathe. Its visor is coated with gold to protect Snoopy from sunlight and small objects.

Under the helmet Snoopy wears a communications carrier assembly, or a "Snoopy cap." It has an earphone and a microphone so astronauts can speak with people.

PEANUTS AND NASA

Snoopy and NASA's relationship began even before the first person walked on the moon. The time line below shows some of the major events in the history of Peanuts and NASA, up until the *Apollo 11* mission.

Charles M. Schulz publishes his first comic strip.

Woodstock appears in the Peanuts comic for the first time.

1950   1958   1967

The National Aeronautics and Space Administration, or NASA, is founded. Its mission was to explore outer space.

NASA creates the Apollo program to send people to the moon.

NASA establishes a Silver Snoopy Award. It is given to outstanding people in the aerospace program. In honor of their work, the award winners receive a silver Snoopy pin that has flown to space.

Apollo 10 launches into space. *Apollo 10*'s mission was to "snoop" around a landing site on the moon, so NASA decided to name the module "Snoopy." They also named the command module "Charlie Brown." The spacecraft also used paintings of Charlie Brown and Snoopy to help focus their camera equipment.

1968 March 1969 May 1969 July 1969

Charles Schulz draws a series of comic strips about Snoopy traveling to the moon.

The *Apollo 11* astronauts become the first humans to land on the moon!

To the moon and beyond!